REUNION

"A minor masterpiece. Uhlman succeeds in lending his narrative a musical quality which is both haunting and lyrical"

ARTHUR KOESTLER

"Melancholy and elegiac with a very effective final twist of the plot" *The Times*

"Finely concise, tender and most painful" *Sunday Times*

FRED UHLMAN was born in Stuttgart, capital of Württemberg in South-West Germany, on 19 January 1901, three days before Queen Victoria died. *Reunion*, written in 1960, is not therefore an autobiographical book, although it contains autobiographical elements. The school, the teachers and the boys are true to life, based on the Eberhard-Ludwig Gymnasium, Württemberg's oldest and most famous grammar school, which the author attended. "The boy in the story is, of course, me," he said, "but I never had any friendship with a 'Hohenfels'. This part is purely fictional, and the Hohenfels are a composite picture of a few aristocratic boys and their parents."

Fred Uhlman claims that it is Württemberg that made him into an artist and a poet, and left him a "Romantic" for life. This beautiful and traditionally democratic region, which includes the Black Forest and Lake Constance, is also the home of many of Germany's greatest poets and thinkers – Schiller, Hölderlin, Mörike, Wieland, Uhland, Schlegel, Hegel, Schelling and Herman Hesse.

This love of his birthplace, which Uhlman, then an anti-Nazi lawyer, had to leave in 1933, illuminates every line of *Reunion*. He died in 1985.

Fred Uhlman

REUNION

With an introduction by
Jean d'Ormesson

THE HARVILL PRESS
LONDON

For Paul and Millicent Bloomfield

First published in Great Britain in 1971 by Adam Books

This paperback edition first published in 1997 by The Harvill Press

3 5 7 9 8 6 4

Copyright © Fred Uhlman, 1971
Introduction copyright © Jean D'Ormesson, 1997
Introduction translation copyright © The Harvill Press, 1997

This paperback edition first published in 1999 by Harvill

The Harvill Press
Random House, 20 Vauxhall Bridge Road, London SW1V 2SA

Random House Australia (Pty) Limited, 20 Alfred Street, Milsons Point
Sydney, New South Wales 2061, Australia

Random House New Zealand Limited, 18 Poland Road, Glenfield
Auckland 10, New Zealand

Random House South Africa (Pty) Limited, Endulini, 5A Jubilee Road
Parktown 2193, South Africa

The Random House Group Limited Reg. No. 954009
www.randomhouse.co.uk/harvill

A CIP catalogue record for this book is available from the British Library

ISBN 1 86046 365 7

Papers used by Random House UK Limited are natural, recyclable products made from wood
grown in sustainable forests. The manufacturing processes conform to the
environmental regulations of the country of origin

Printed and bound in Great Britain by Bookmarque Ltd, Croydon, Surrey

INTRODUCTION

I REMEMBER AS IF it were yesterday my first encounter, some twenty years ago, with this small volume, brought to my attention by a friend. Delight and distress mingled in me so powerfully that I found myself smiling through tears that came to my eyes. My vision blurred and it was impossible to continue, a great happiness overcame me. It was as if, amid the flames of hell, angels had started to sing.

Only two or three times in the course of my life had I felt so stunned. With Isaac B. Singer perhaps, *The Crown of Feathers*; with good old Hemingway's *The Sun Also Rises*, and Aragon's bizarre tale, *Le Paysan de Paris*, written during his youthful surrealist period before he turned to communism. At that time I was discussing books on television. I rushed onto the programme to announce, as forcefully as I could, that I had come upon a masterpiece written by a painter of German origin who lived in England.

The book had enormous success in France. First because of obvious qualities that nobody could miss, its literary perfection. Also, I think, because every reader was as anxious as I was to meet the author and to hug him to their heart.

The most admirable feature, I believe, in Fred Uhlman's book is the conjunction of two adventures of unequal weight – an adolescent friendship and the rise of Nazism – where both of them are charged with the same emotion. The two themes are treated with a simple delicacy of touch that is quite enchanting, and to have set them forth so lucidly is an accomplishment that borders on the miraculous.

The book begins like Flaubert's *Madame Bovary*, plunging us straightaway into the magical world of the very last days of childhood and the troubled beginnings of adolescence. A pupil arrives in a new class: "He came into my life in February 1932 and never left it again." At once destiny, childhood love and teenage friendship set up a tingle in one's spine.

Young Conrad von Hohenfels is as handsome and charming as a god; he befriends Hans Schwarz, the narrator, son of a Jewish doctor and grandson of a rabbi. Impossible, it seems to me, not to think at once of bonds forged elsewhere and in other circumstances, namely those that bind Charles Swann and the Guermantes in Proust. As with Swann and the Guermantes, young Schwarz is dazzled by the aura that surrounds the Hohenfels, and his friendship with Conrad takes a passionate turn, described by Uhlman with exquisite tact. The rabbi's grandson keeps some priceless treasures in his room – a lion's tooth, three Greek coins, an elephant's molar, a Roman tile with the inscription LEG XI; he cannot wait to show them to his new friend, one of whose forbears had tried, albeit in vain, to save Frederick Barbarossa from drowning in the Cydnus and another of whom had died at Salerno in the arms of Frederick II Hohenstaufen, nicknamed *Stupor mundi*.

Here is the purest story of adolescence and friendship,

between two boys whom History separates and ultimately destroys. Hitler is about to seize power, the most crass and barbaric savagery is about to ravage the land of Goethe and of Hölderlin. By the simplest words, which weigh more heavily than any amount of indignation or imprecation, we are set on the ineluctable path that leads to one of the most horrible catastrophes to afflict mankind. Conrad von Hohenfels' mother sides with Hitler. Hans Schwarz's parents commit suicide. Germany, her honour in shreds, is destroyed. Hans Schwartz survives the disaster by leaving for America.

The book's ending, in a few lines, is a masterpiece within the masterpiece. It transforms, suddenly, what has been a long short story into a novel of epic dimensions; it adds a further luminous, dramatic quality, like the swell of an organ, to what has been a *Bildungsroman*, a story of growing-up, while retaining the powerful grace and simplicity of the short story. In the closing lines I gave up the fight; I wept buckets. No matter – it was the end.

Perhaps I may be allowed to insert a brief personal note. Throughout the era in which Fred Uhlman's masterpiece is set, my father was a diplomat in Germany. He loathed Hitler. He saved many Jews like Hans Schwarz and his parents. He was also at ease in the milieu frequented by the Hohenfels which Uhlman depicts so well. I have the feeling that I grew up – I would have been six or seven – there in Uhlman's novel and that its characters leaned over my little cot near the banks of the Isar in person. As I read Uhlman, as I followed, my heart in my mouth, the crossed destinies of Schwarz and the Hohenfels, I thought of my father. And my tears flowed the more freely.

And my joy, too. What is splendid, what is matchless in Fred Uhlman's book is that it shows man's baseness, stupidity and cruelty to be inseparable from his greatness and integrity. The book plunges us into sorrow and horror, and in the last line it restores to us our reasons for hope. This is what these few pages by a German Jewish painter, who lived in England, has in common with the great constructions of Dante, of Shakespeare, of Milton or of Pascal: the worst is not always to be counted on, and amid the accursed there are always the just and these, at the last moment, God snatches from the darkness.

Jean d'Ormesson, 1997

REUNION

I

HE CAME INTO my life in February 1932 and never left it again. More than a quarter of a century has passed since then, more than nine thousand days, desultory and tedious, hollow with the sense of effort or work without hope – days and years, many of them as dead as dry leaves on a dead tree.

I can remember the day and the hour when I first set eyes on this boy who was to be the source of my greatest happiness and of my greatest despair. It was two days after my sixteenth birthday at three o'clock in the afternoon on a grey, dark, German winter's day. I was at the Karl Alexander Gymnasium in Stuttgart, Württemberg's most famous grammar school, founded in 1521, the year when Luther stood before Charles V, Holy Roman Emperor and king of Spain.

I remember every detail: the classroom with its heavy benches and tables, the sour, musty odour of forty damp winter overcoats, the puddles of melted snow, the brownish-yellow lines on the grey walls where once, before the revolution, the pictures of Kaiser Wilhelm and the King of Württemberg had hung. If I shut my eyes I can still see the backs of my schoolmates, many of whom perished later on the Russian steppes or in the sands of Alamein. I can still hear the tired, disillusioned voice of Herr Zimmermann, who was condemned to teaching for life and had accepted his fate with sad resignation. He was a sallow-faced man, whose hair, moustache and sharply pointed beard were all tinged with grey. He looked out at the world through a pince-nez on the tip of his nose with the expression of a mongrel dog in search of food. Though he was probably not more than fifty years old to us he seemed to be eighty. We despised him because he was kind and gentle and because he had a poor man's smell – his two-roomed flat probably had no bath – and he was dressed in a much patched, shiny, greenish suit which he wore during the autumn and the long, winter months (he had a second suit for spring and summer). We treated him with contempt and occasionally with cruelty, the cowardly cruelty which so many healthy boys show towards the weak, the old and the defenceless.

It was getting dark, but not dark enough for the lights to go on, and through the windows I could still clearly see the garrison church, an ugly late nineteenth-century building made beautiful now by the snow covering its twin towers which pierced the leaden sky. Beautiful too were the white hills that enclosed my home town, beyond which the world seemed to end and mystery to begin. I was half asleep and half awake, doodling, dreaming, occasionally pulling a hair out of my head to keep myself awake, when there was a knock at the door, and before Herr Zimmermann could say "*Herein*" in came Professor Klett, the Headmaster. But nobody looked at the dapper little man, for all eyes were turned towards the stranger who followed him as Phaedrus might have followed Socrates.

We stared at him as if we had seen a ghost. What struck me and probably all of us more than anything else, more than his self-assured bearing, his aristocratic air and slight, faintly supercilious smile, was his elegance. We were all, so far as our style of dress was concerned, a dreary lot. Most of our mothers felt that anything was good enough for us to go to school in, so long as it was made of a tough, durable fabric. We weren't as yet very interested in girls, so we didn't mind being dressed in the functional, hard-wearing assortment of jackets and short trousers or breeches bought for us in the hope that they would last till we grew out of them.

But with this boy it was different. He wore *long* trousers, beautifully cut and creased, obviously not off the peg like ours. His suit looked expensive: it was light grey with a herringbone pattern and almost certainly "Guaranteed English". He wore a pale blue shirt and a dark blue tie with small white polka-dots; in contrast our neckwear was dirty, greasy and rope-like. Even though we regarded any attempt at elegance as "sissy", we couldn't help looking enviously at this picture of ease and distinction.

Professor Klett went straight to Herr Zimmermann, whispered something in his ear, and disappeared without being noticed by us because our eyes were concentrated on the Newcomer. He stood motionless and composed, without any sign of nervousness or shyness. Somehow he looked older than us and more mature, and it was difficult to believe he was just another new boy. It wouldn't have surprised us if he had disappeared as silently and mysteriously as he had come in.

Herr Zimmermann moved his pince-nez higher up his nose, searched the classroom with tired eyes, discovered an empty seat just in front of me, stepped down from his dais and – to the amazement of the class – accompanied the Newcomer to his appointed place. Then, slightly inclining his head, as if he had half a mind to bow but didn't quite dare, walked slowly backwards, facing the stranger all the time. Climbing back on to his seat, he addressed him: "Would you please give me your surname, Christian name and the date and place of your birth?"

The young man stood up. "Graf von Hohenfels, Konradin," he announced, "born on the 19th January 1916, Burg Hohenfels, Württemberg." Then he sat down.

2

I STARED AT this strange boy, who was exactly my own age, as if he had come from another world. It wasn't because he was a count. There were quite a few "vons" in my class, but they seemed no different from the rest of us who were sons of merchants, bankers, pastors, tailors or railway officials. There was Freiherr von Gall, a poor little chap, son of a retired Army officer who could only afford margarine for his children. There was Baron von Waldeslust, whose father had a Burg near Wimpfen-am-Neckar, and whose ancestor had been ennobled for rendering services of a questionable nature to Duke Eberhard Ludwig. We even had a Prince Hubertus Schleim – Gleim – Lichtenstein, but he was so stupid that even his princely descent couldn't save him from being a laughing stock.

But this was different. The Hohenfels were part of our history. It was true that their Burg, situated between Hohenstaufen, the Teck and Hohenzollern, was in ruins, the towers destroyed, leaving the cone of the mountain bare, but their fame was still green. I knew their deeds as well as those of Scipio Africanus or Hannibal or Caesar.

Hildebrandt von Hohenfels died in 1190 trying to save Frederick I of Hohenstaufen, the great Barbarossa, from the swift-flowing river Calycadnus in Asia Minor. Anno von Hohenfels was the friend of Frederick II, most magnificent of the Hohenstaufens, Stupor Mundi, whose book *De arte venandi cum avibus* he had helped to write, and who died at Salerno in the year 1247 in the arms of the Emperor. (His body still rests in Catania in a porphyry sarcophagus supported by four lions.) Frederick von Hohenfels, buried in Kloster Hirschau, was killed at Pavia after taking Francis I of France prisoner. Waldemar von Hohenfels fell at Leipzig. Two brothers, Fritz and Ulrich, lost their lives at Champigny in 1871, the younger first, the elder while trying to carry him to safety. Another Frederick von Hohenfels was killed at Verdun.

And here, only a foot or two away, sat a member of this illustrious Swabian family, sharing the same room with me, under my observant, spellbound eyes. Every movement he made interested me: how he opened his polished satchel, how, with his white, spotlessly clean hands (so different from mine which were short, clumsy and ink-stained) he laid out his fountain pen and arrow-sharp pencils, and how he opened and shut his notebook. Everything about him aroused my curiosity: the care with which he selected his pencil, the way he sat – erect, as if at any moment he might have to get up and give an order to an invisible army – and how he stroked his blond hair. I only relaxed when he, like everyone else, got bored and fidgeted whilst waiting for the bell for the interval between lessons. I studied his proud, finely carved face, and indeed no lover could have watched Helen of Troy more intently or could have been more convinced of his own inferiority. Who was *I* to dare to talk to him? In which of Europe's ghettos had my ancestors been huddled when Frederick von Hohenstaufen gave Anno von Hohenfels his bejewelled hand? What could I, son of a Jewish doctor, grandson and great-grandson of a Rabbi, and of a line of small merchants and cattle dealers, offer this golden-haired boy whose very name filled me with such awe?

How would he in all his glory ever be able to understand my shyness, my suspicious pride and my fear of being hurt? What had he, Konradin von Hohenfels, in common with me, Hans Schwarz, so wanting in self-assurance and fashionable graces?

Strangely enough, I wasn't the only one too nervous to talk to him. Nearly all the boys seemed to avoid him. Normally rough and uncouth in word and deed, always ready to call each other disgusting nicknames, Smelly, Stinker, Sausage, Pigface or Swine, pushing each other around with or without provocation, they were all silent and embarrassed in his presence, giving way to him whenever he got up and wherever he went. They too seemed to be under some spell. If I or anyone else had dared to turn up dressed like Hohenfels, we would have been exposed to merciless ridicule. Even Herr Zimmermann seemed afraid of disturbing him.

And there was another thing. *His* homework was corrected with the greatest care. Where Zimmermann would only write in the margin of my paper short remarks like "Badly constructed", "What does this mean?" or "Not too bad", "More care, please", *his* work was corrected with a wealth of observations and explanations which must have cost our teacher many minutes of extra labour.

He didn't seem to mind being left to himself. Perhaps he was used to it. But he never gave the slightest impression of pride or vanity or of having any conscious wish to be different from the rest of us. Except that, unlike us, he was always extremely polite, smiling when anyone spoke to him, actually holding the door open when someone wanted to leave the room. And yet somehow the boys seemed afraid of him. I can only imagine that it was the Hohenfels mystique which made them, like myself, shy and self-conscious.

Even the Prince and the Baron left him alone at first, but a week after his arrival I saw all the "vons" approach him during the interval after the second lesson. The

Prince spoke to him, then the Baron and the Freiherr. I could only hear a few words: "My aunt Hohenlohe", "Maxie said" (who was Maxie?). More names were dropped, obviously familiar to them all. Some caused general merriment, others were mentioned with every sign of respect and almost whispered as if royalty were present. But this *rencontre* didn't seem to lead to anything. When they met again they nodded and smiled and exchanged a few words, but Konradin seemed as aloof as before.

A few days later it was the turn of the "Caviar" of the class. Three boys, Reutter, Müller and Frank, were known by this sobriquet because they kept strictly to themselves in the belief that they, and they alone among us, were destined to make their mark in the world. They went to plays and operas, read Baudelaire, Rimbaud and Rilke, talked about paranoia and the id, admired *Dorian Gray* and *The Forsyte Saga*, and of course each other. Frank's father was a rich industrialist and they foregathered regularly at his house where they met a few actors and actresses, a painter who from time to time went to Paris to see "my friend Pablo", and several ladies with literary ambitions and connections. They were allowed to smoke and they called the actresses by their Christian names.

After having unanimously decided that a von Hohenfels would be an asset to their coterie they approached him – though with some trepidation. Frank, the least nervous of them, stopped him as he was leaving the class and stammered something about "our little salon", about poetry readings, the need to defend oneself against the *profanum vulgus*, and added that they would be honoured if he would join their *Literaturbund*. Hohenfels, who had never heard of the Caviar, smiled politely, said something about being terribly busy "just now" and left the three wise men frustrated.

3

I CAN'T REMEMBER exactly when I decided that Konradin had to be my friend, but that one day he *would* be my friend I didn't doubt. Until his arrival I had been without a friend. There wasn't one boy in my class who I believed could live up to my romantic ideal of friendship, not one whom I really admired, for whom I would have been willing to die and who could have understood my demand for complete trust, loyalty and self-sacrifice. All of them struck me as more or less clumsy, rather commonplace, healthy and unimaginative Swabians — even the Caviar lot seemed no exception. Most of the boys were pleasant and I got on well enough with them. But just as I had no particularly strong feelings for them, so they had none for me. I never visited their homes and they never came to our house. Perhaps another reason for my coolness was that they all appeared to be so immensely practical, and already knew what they wanted to be, lawyers, officers, teachers, pastors and bankers. I alone had no idea, only vague dreams and even vaguer desires. All I knew was that I wanted to travel, and I believed that one day I would be a great poet.

I hesitated before writing down "a friend for whom I would have been willing to die". But even after thirty years I believe this was no exaggeration and that I would have been ready to die for a friend – almost glad. Just as I took it for granted that it was *dulce et decorum pro Germania mori*, so I would have agreed that to die *pro amico* was *dulce et decorum* too. Between the ages of sixteen and eighteen boys sometimes combine a naïve innocence, a radiant purity of body and mind, with a passionate urge to absolute and selfless devotion. The phase usually only lasts a short time, but because of its intensity and uniqueness it remains one of life's most precious experiences.

4

ALL I KNEW, then, was that he was going to be my friend. Everything attracted me to him. First and foremost the glory of his name which singled him out – for me – from all the other boys, including the "vons" (just as I would have been more attracted by the Duchesse de Guermantes than by a Madame Meunier). Then his proud bearing, his manners, his elegance, his good looks – and who could be altogether insensitive to them? – powerfully suggested to me that here at last I had found someone who came up to my ideal of a friend.

The problem was how to attract him to me. What could I offer the one who had gently but firmly turned down the aristocrats and the Caviar? How could I conquer him, entrenched behind barriers of tradition, his natural pride and acquired arrogance? Moreover he seemed quite content to be alone and to stay aloof from the other boys, with whom he mixed only because he had to.

How to attract his attention, how to impress him with the fact that I was different from this dull crowd, how to convince him that I alone ought to be his friend – this was a problem for which I had no clear answer. All I knew instinctively was that I had to *stand out*. Suddenly I began to take a new interest in what was going on in class. Normally I was happy to be left alone with my dreams, undisturbed by question or problems, waiting for the bell to release me from drudgery. There had been no particular reason why I should impress my schoolmates. As long as I passed my exams, which didn't give me much difficulty, why exert myself? Why impress the teachers? Those tired, disillusioned old men who used to tell us that *non scholae sed vitae discimus* when it seemed to me that it was the other way round?

But now I came to life. I jumped up whenever I felt I had anything to say. I discussed *Madame Bovary*, and the existence or non-existence of Homer, I attacked Schiller, called Heine a poet for commercial travellers and made Hölderlin out to be Germany's greatest poet, "even greater than Goethe". Looking back I see how childish it all was – yet I certainly electrified my teachers and even the Caviar took notice. The results also surprised me. The masters, who had given me up, suddenly felt that their efforts hadn't been wasted after all, and that at last they were getting some reward for their labour. They turned to me with renewed hope and a touching, almost pathetic joy. They asked me to translate and to explain scenes from *Faust* and *Hamlet*, which I did with real pleasure and, I like to believe, some understanding. My second determined effort came during the few hours dedicated to physical exercise. At that time – perhaps it's different today – our teachers at the Karl Alexander Gymnasium considered sport a luxury. To chase or to hit a ball, as was the habit in America and Britain, seemed to them a terrible waste of valuable time that could be more beneficially devoted to acquiring knowledge. Two hours a week to strengthen one's body was regarded as adequate, if not more than enough. Our gym instructor was a noisy, tough little man, Max Loehr, known as Muscle Max, who was desperately keen on developing our chests and arms and legs as intensively as possible in the short time at his disposal. In this cause he employed three internationally notorious instruments of torture – the Horizontal Bar, the Parallel Bars and the Vaulting Horse. The usual form was a run round the hall, then some bending and stretching. After this warming-up Muscle Max would go to his favourite instrument of the three, the Horizontal Bar, and show us a few exercises, as easy for him as falling off a log, but for most of us extremely difficult. Usually he would ask one of the most agile boys to emulate his performance and sometimes he picked on me, but in the last months he had more often called on Eisemann, who loved showing off and anyway wanted to be a Reichswehr officer.

This time I was determined to get my oar in. Muscle Max went back to the Horizontal Bar, stood to attention under it, stretched up his arms and then jumped elegantly, grasping the rod in his iron grip. With incredible ease and skill he raised his body slowly, inch by inch, up to the bar until it rested there. Then he turned to the right, stretched both arms out, back to the old position, turned to the left, and back to rest. But suddenly he seemed to fall, for a moment he hung suspended by his knees, his hands almost touching the floor. Slowly he started swinging, faster and faster, till he was back at his place on the bar and then, with a quick, magnificent movement, he launched himself into the void and landed with the lightest of thuds on his toes. His expertise made the feat seem easy, though in fact it needed complete control, a wonderful balance and also nerve. Of the three qualities, I had something of the first two, but I can't say I was very brave. Often at the last moment I doubted if I could do it. I hardly dared let go, and when I did it never entered my head that I should do it nearly as well as Muscle Max. It was the difference between a juggler able to keep six balls in the air and somebody thankful to be able to manage three.

On this particular occasion I stepped forward as soon as Max had finished his demonstration and stared him straight in the eyes. He hesitated for a second, and then "Schwarz", he said.

I walked slowly to the bar, stood to attention and jumped. My body, like his, rested on the rod. I looked round. I saw Max below me, ready for any slip-up. The boys stood quiet and watched me. I looked at Hohenfels and when I saw his eyes focused on me I raised my body from right to left and from left to right, hung on my knees, swung upwards and rested for a second on the bar. I had no fear, only one will and one desire. I was going to do it for him. Suddenly I raised my body right up, jumped over the bar, flew in the air – and then *thump*!

At least I was on my feet.

There were some suppressed giggles, but a few of the boys clapped; they weren't such bad fellows, some of them . . .

Standing quite still I looked at *him*. Needless to say Konradin hadn't giggled. He hadn't clapped either. But he looked at *me*.

A few days later, I came to school with a few Greek coins – I had been collecting coins since I was twelve. I brought a Corinthian silver drachma, an owl of Pallas Athene, a head of Alexander the Great, and as soon as he approached his place, I pretended to be studying them through a magnifying glass. He saw me looking at them and, as I had hoped, his curiosity got the better of his restraint. He asked me if he might look at them too. From the way he handled the coins I could see he knew something about them; he had the collector's way of fondling the beloved objects and the collector's appreciative, caressing look. He told me he collected coins too, and that he had the owl but didn't have my head of Alexander. He also had some coins which I hadn't.

Here we were interrupted by the entrance of the teacher, and by the ten o'clock interval Konradin seemed to have lost interest and left the room without even looking at me. Still, I felt happy. It was the first time he had talked to me and I was determined it should not be the last.

5

THREE DAYS LATER, on March 15th – I shall always remember the date – I was going home from school. It was a soft, cool, spring evening. The almond trees were in full bloom, the crocuses were out and the sky was pastel blue and sea green, a northern sky with a touch of Italy. I saw Hohenfels in front of me and he seemed to hesitate and to be waiting for somebody. I slowed down – I was afraid of overtaking him – but I had to go on, for it would have looked ridiculous not to and he might have misunderstood my hesitation. When I had almost reached him he turned and smiled at me. Then, with a strangely gauche and still hesitant movement, he shook my trembling hand. "Hello, Hans," he said, and suddenly I realized to my joy and relief and amazement that he was as shy and as much in need of a friend as I.

I can't remember much of what Konradin said to me that day or what I said to him. All I know is that we walked up and down for an hour, like two young lovers, still nervous, still afraid of each other; but somehow I knew that this was only a beginning and that from now on my life would no longer be empty and dull but full of hope and richness for us both.

When at last I left him I ran all the way home. I laughed, I talked to myself, I wanted to shout and sing, and I found it very difficult not to tell my parents how happy I was, that my whole life had changed, and that I was no longer a beggar but as rich as Croesus. Fortunately my parents were too preoccupied to notice the change in me. They were used to my moody and bored expressions, my evasive answers and my prolonged silences which they attributed to "growing pains" and the mysterious transition from adolescence to manhood. Occasionally my mother had tried to penetrate my defences, once or twice she had tried to stroke my hair, but she had given this up long ago, discouraged by my stubbornness and lack of response.

But later a reaction set in. I slept badly, because I was afraid of the morning. Perhaps he had already forgotten me or regretted his surrender? Perhaps it had been a mistake to let him feel how much I needed his friendship? Should I have been more cautious, more reserved? Perhaps he had told his parents about me and they had warned him against chumming up with a Jew? So I went on torturing myself until at last I fell into a restless sleep.

6

BUT ALL MY fears proved to be groundless. As soon
as I went into the classroom Konradin came straight up
and sat next to me. His pleasure at seeing me was so
genuine, so unmistakable, that even I, with my inbred
suspicions, lost all fear. It was clear to me from what he
said that he had slept extremely well, and that not for a
moment had he doubted my sincerity, and I felt ashamed
of ever having suspected him.

From this day on we were inseparable. We always
left school together – our homes were in the same
direction – and he waited for me in the mornings. The
class, amazed to begin with, soon took our friendship
for granted except for Bollacher, who later nicknamed
us Castor and Pollack, and the Caviar, who decided
to cut us.

The next few months were the happiest of my life.
Spring came and the whole country was one mass of
blossoms, cherry and apple, pear and peach, while the
poplars took on their silver and the willows their lemon
yellow. The soft, serene bluish hills of Swabia were
covered with vineyards and orchards and crowned with

castles; and these small medieval towns had high gabled town halls, and from their fountains, standing on pillars and surrounded by water-spouting monsters, there looked down stiff comic, heavily-armed and mustachioed Swabian dukes, or counts with names like Eberhardt the Well-beloved or Ulrich the Terrible; and the Neckar flowed gently round willowy isles. All of this conveyed a feeling of peace, of trust in the present and hope for the future.

On Saturdays Konradin and I used to take a slow train and go and spend the night in one of many old heavily-timbered inns, where one could get a cheap, clean room, excellent food and local wine. Sometimes we went to the Black Forest where the dark woods, smelling of mushrooms and the tears of amber-coloured mastic, were threaded through by trout streams with sawmills on their banks. Sometimes we wandered on as far as the mountain tops and in the bluish distance one could see the valley of the quick-flowing Rhine, the lavender-blue Vosges and the spire of Strasbourg cathedral. Or the Neckar would tempt us with

gentle breezes, heralds of Italy

And you with all your poplars, beloved river

or the Danube with its

trees enough, white-flowering and reddish and darker ones, wild, full of dark green leaves.

Sometimes we chose the Hegau, where there were seven extinct volcanoes, or the Lake of Constance, dreamiest of all lakes. Once we went to Hohenstaufen and Teck and Hohenfels. Not a stone of those strongholds remained, nor any track to mark the road the Crusaders had followed to Byzantium and Jerusalem. A short distance away was Tübingen, where Hölderlin-Hyperion, the poet we loved best, had spent thirty-six years of his life out of his mind, *entrückt von den Göttern*, swept up by the Gods. Looking down on the tower, Hölderlin's home, his gentle prison, we would recite our favourite poem:

> Hung with yellow pears
> And with wild roses loaded
> The land is mirrored in the lake.
> You sweet swans,
> Drunk with kisses
> You dip your head
> In the sacred, sober water.
>
> Ah me, where can I seek
> In winter the flowers
> And where sunshine
> And shadow of earth?
> The walls stand
> Speechless and cold, in the wind
> Icy flags tinkle.

7

AND SO THE days and months passed by and nothing disturbed our friendship. From outside our magic circle came rumours of political unrest, but the storm-centre was far away – in Berlin, whence clashes were reported between Nazis and Communists. Stuttgart seemed to be as quiet and reasonable as ever. It is true that there were occasional minor incidents – swastikas appeared on walls, a Jewish citizen was molested, a few Communists were beaten up – but life in general went on as usual. The *Höhenrestaurants*, the Opera and the open-air cafés were packed. The weather was hot, the vineyards were full of grapes, and the apple trees began to bend under the weight of the ripening fruit. People talked about where they were going for their summer holidays; my parents mentioned Switzerland, and Konradin told me he would be joining his father and mother in Sicily. There seemed to be nothing to worry about. Politics were the business of grown-up people; we had our own problems to solve. And of these we thought the most urgent was to learn how to make the best use of life, quite apart from discovering what purpose, if any, life had and what the human condition would be in this frightening and immeasurable cosmos. These were questions of real and eternal significance, far more important to us than the existence of such ephemeral and ridiculous figures as Hitler and Mussolini.

Then something happened that shook us both and had a great effect on me.

Until then I had taken for granted the existence of an all-powerful and benevolent God, creator of the universe. My father never spoke to me about religion, leaving it to me to believe in whatever I liked. I once overheard him saying to my mother that, in spite of the lack of contemporary evidence, he believed a historical Jesus had existed, a Jewish teacher of morals, of great wisdom and gentleness, a prophet like Jeremiah or Ezekiel, but that he could not for his life understand how anybody could regard this Jesus as "Son of God". He found blasphemous and repellent the conception of an omnipotent God who could passively watch His Son suffer that bitter and lingering death on the cross, a Divine "Father" with less than a human father's urge to come to his child's assistance.

Still, although my father had expressed his disbelief in Christ's divinity, I think his views were agnostic rather than atheistic and that if I had wanted to become a Christian he wouldn't have objected – no more, for that matter, than if I had wanted to become a Buddhist. On the other hand, I'm pretty sure that he would have tried to prevent me from becoming a monk of any persuasion, because he would have regarded the monastic and contemplative life as irrational and wasteful.

As for my mother, she seemed to drift along perfectly content in a state of muddle. She went to the synagogue on the Day of Atonement, but would sing "Stille Nacht, Heilige Nacht" at Christmas. She used to give money to the Jews for the assistance of Jewish children in Poland, and to the Christians for the conversion of Jews to Christianity. When I was a child she taught me a few simple prayers in which I begged God to help me to be good to Daddy, Mummy and our pussy-cat. But this was about all. Like my father, she didn't seem to need any religion, but she was busy, kind and generous, and convinced that their son would be sure to follow their example. And so I grew up among Jews and Christians, left to myself and with my own ideas about God, neither deeply believing nor seriously doubting that there was a benevolent master-mind over all and that our world was the unique centre of the universe and that we, Jews and Gentiles, were God's favourite children.

Now our neighbours were a Mr and Mrs Bauer who had two girls, aged four and seven, and a boy of twelve. I didn't know them very well – the children had been too young for me to play with – but I knew them by sight, and had often noticed, not without envy, how parents and children romped together in the garden. I remember vividly how the father pushed one of the little girls, who sat on a swing, higher and higher, and how the white of her dress and her reddish hair looked like a burning candle swiftly moving between the fresh, pale-green leaves of the apple trees.

One night, when the parents were out and the maid had gone on an errand, the wooden house roared up in flames so mercilessly fast that before the fire engines could get there the children had been burnt to death. I didn't see the fire or hear the screams of the maid and the mother. I only heard about it next day when I saw the blackened walls, the burnt dolls, and the charred ropes of the swing dangling like snakes from the shrivelled tree.

It shook me as nothing had shaken me before. I had heard about earthquakes that engulfed thousands, about streams of burning lava that buried villages, about oceans that swallowed up islands. I had read of one million people drowned by the Yellow River, of two million drowned by the Yangtse. I knew that a million soldiers died at Verdun. But these were mere abstractions – numbers, statistics, information. One couldn't suffer for a million.

But these three children I knew, I had seen with my own eyes – this was altogether different. What had they done, what had the poor mother and the father done to deserve this?

It seemed to me that there were just two possibilities. Either no God existed, or there did exist a deity who was monstrous if powerful and futile if powerless. Once and for all I jettisoned all belief in a benevolent mastermind.

I spoke out about this in passionate and despairing outbursts to my friend. He, brought up in the strict Protestant faith, refused to accept what then seemed to me the only possible logical conclusion: that no divine father existed or that if he did exist, he cared nothing for mankind and in consequence was as useless as any pagan god. Konradin agreed that what had happened was terrible, and that he could find no explanation for it. But surely, he persisted, there must be an answer, only we were just too young and inexperienced to find it. Such catastrophes had been happening for millions of years, men far wiser and more intelligent than ourselves, priests, bishops and saints, had discussed it and had found explanations. We should accept their superior wisdom and be humbly submissive.

I rejected all this fiercely, told him that I didn't care what all those fraudulent old men had to say, that nothing, absolutely nothing, could explain or excuse the burning of two small girls and one little boy. "Can't you see them burning?" I shouted in despair. "Can't you hear their screams? And you have the cheek to defend it because you aren't brave enough to live without your God. What use to you or me is a powerless, pitiless God? A God sitting in the clouds and condoning malaria and cholera, famine and war?"

Konradin said that he himself could give no rational explanation but that he would ask his pastor, and a few days later he came back reassured. What I had said was the outpouring of a schoolboy's immature and untrained mind, and he had been told not to listen to such blasphemy. The pastor had answered all his questions fully and satisfactorily.

But either the pastor hadn't explained clearly enough or Konradin hadn't understood the explanation – at any rate he couldn't make it clear to me. He spoke a lot about evil, and about it being necessary if we were to appreciate good, just as there was no beauty without ugliness, but he failed to convince me and our discussions ended in deadlock.

It happened that just then I was for the first time reading about light years, nebulae, galaxies; about suns thousands of times bigger than our sun, millions or billions of stars, planets thousands of times the size of Mars and Venus, Jupiter and Saturn. And for the first time I realized vividly that I was a particle of dust, and that our earth was no more than a pebble on a beach with millions of such pebbles. This was grist to my mill. It served to reinforce my belief that there was no God – how could he possibly take an interest in what was going on in so many celestial bodies? And this new discovery, combined with the shock of the children's death, led, after a period of complete despair, to one of intense curiosity. Now the crucial question no longer seemed to be what life was, but what one was to do with this value-less, yet somehow uniquely valuable life. How should one spend it? To what end? For our own good alone? For the good of mankind? How was one to make the best of this bad job?

All this we discussed almost daily, walking solemnly up and down the streets of Stuttgart, often looking up to the sky, to Betelgeuse and Aldebaran which looked back at us with glittering, ice-blue, mocking, millions-of-light-years-removed snake's eyes.

But this was only one of the subjects we thrashed out. There were secular interests too, which seemed far more important than the certainty of the extinction of our earth, still millions of years away, and of our own death, which then seemed even more remote. There was our common interest in books and poetry, our discovery of art, the impact of Post Impressionism and Expressionism, the theatre, the opera.

And we talked about girls. By today's standards of

adolescent sophistication our attitude was incredibly naïve. To us, girls were superior beings of fabulous purity, to be approached only as the troubadours approached them, with chivalrous fervour and distant adoration.

I knew very few girls. At home I occasionally saw two teenage cousins, dull creatures, without the slightest resemblance to Andromeda or Antigone. One of them I only remember because she never stopped stuffing herself with chocolate cake, and the other because she seemed to lose her voice as soon as I appeared. Konradin was luckier. At least he met girls with exciting names like Gräfin von Platow, Baroness von Henkel Donnersmark, and even a Jeanne de Montmorency who, he confessed to me, had more than once appeared to him in dreams.

At school there wasn't much talk about girls. This, anyhow, was our impression (Konradin's and mine) although there might have been all sorts of goings-on without our knowing, since we two, like the Caviar, kept very much to ourselves. But looking back I still think that most of the boys, even the ones who boasted about their adventures, were rather afraid of girls. As yet there was no television to bring sex into the bosom of the family.

But I am not concerned to assess the merits of such innocence as ours, which I only mention as one aspect of our life together. What I am trying to do by recounting our main interests, sorrows, joys and problems is to recapture and try to communicate our state of mind.

Our problems we tried to solve alone and unaided. It never occurred to us to consult our parents. They belonged, we were convinced, to another world, and would either not understand us or refuse to take us seriously. We hardly ever talked about them; they seemed as far away as the nebulae, too grown up, too crystallized in conventions of one sort or another. Konradin knew that my father was a doctor and I that his father had been Ambassador to Turkey and Brazil, but we weren't curious to know more, and this perhaps explained why we had never been to each other's homes. Many of our discussions took place as we walked up and down the streets, sat on benches or stood in doorways taking shelter from the rain.

One day, as we were standing outside my house, it occurred to me that Konradin had never seen my room, my books and collections, so I said to him – on the spur of the moment – "Why don't you come in?"

He hesitated for a second, not having expected my invitation, but followed me.

8

MY PARENTS' HOUSE, a modest villa built of
local stone, stood in a small garden full of cherry and
apple trees in what was locally known as *die Höhenlage* of
Stuttgart. Here were the houses of the well-off or rich
bourgeoisie of the place, one of the most beautiful and
prosperous towns in Germany. Surrounded by hills
and vineyards, it lies in a valley so narrow that there
are only a few streets on level ground; most of them start
climbing up the hills as soon as one leaves the
Königstrasse, Stuttgart's main street. Looking down from
the hills one has a remarkable view: thousands of villas,
the old and new *Schloss*, the *Stiftskirche*, the Opera,
museums and what were Royal parks. *Höhenrestaurants*
were everywhere, with large terraces where the people
of Stuttgart could spend the hot summer evenings,
drinking Neckar or Rhine wine and stuffing themselves
with enormous quantities of food: veal and potato salad,
Schnitzel Holstein, Bodenseefelchen, trout from the Black
Forest, hot liver and blood sausages with sauerkraut,
Rehrücken with *Preiselbeeren,* tournedos sauce Béarnaise,
God alone knows what else, followed by a fantastic

choice of rich cakes topped with whipped cream. If they troubled to look up from their food they could see, between trees and laurel bushes, the forests stretching away for miles and the Neckar flowing slowly along between cliffs, castles, poplar trees, vineyards and ancient towns towards Heidelberg, the Rhine and the North Sea. When night fell the view was as magic as looking down from Fiesole on Florence: thousands of lights, the air hot and fragrant with the smell of jasmine and lilac, and on all sides the voices, the singing and laughter of contented citizens, getting rather sleepy from too much food, or amorous from too much drink.

Down in the sweltering town the streets bore names which reminded the Swabians of their rich heritage: Hölderlin, Schiller, Möricke, Uhland, Wieland, Hegel, Schelling, David Friedrich Strauss, Hesse, confirming them in their conviction that outside Württemberg life was hardly worth living, and that no Bavarian, Saxon or least of all Prussian, could hold a candle to them. And this pride was not altogether unjustified. This town of less than half a million inhabitants had more opera, better theatre, finer museums, richer collections and a fuller life than Manchester or Birmingham, Bordeaux or Toulouse. It was still a capital even without a king, surrounded by prosperous small towns and castles with names like Sanssouci and Monrepos: not far away were

Hohenstaufen and Teck and Hohenzollern and the Black Forest, and the Bodensee, the monasteries of Maulbronn and Beuron, the Baroque churches of Zwiefalten, Neresheim and Birnau.

9

FROM OUR HOUSE I could see only the gardens and
red roofs of the villas whose owners were better off than
we were and could afford a view, but my father was
determined that one day we would get even with the
patrician families. Meanwhile we had to make do with
our centrally-heated house with its four bedrooms,
dining room, "Winter garden" and one room which was
used as my father's surgery.

My room was on the second floor and furnished to
my own taste. On the walls were a few reproductions:
Cézanne's *The Boy in a Red Waistcoat*, a few Japanese
woodcuts and the *Sunflowers* by Van Gogh. Then books:
the German classics, Schiller, Kleist, Goethe, Hölderlin,
and of course "our" Shakespeare as well as Rilke, Dehmel
and George. My collection of French books included
Baudelaire, Balzac, Flaubert and Stendhal and of the
Russians the whole of Dostoevsky, Tolstoy and Gogol. In
a corner under glass were my collections: coins, rose-red
corals, bloodstone and agate, topaz, garnet, malachite, a
lump of lava from Herculaneum, a lion's tooth, a tiger's
claw, a piece of sealskin, a Roman fibula, two fragments of

Roman glass (pinched from a museum), a Roman tile with the inscription LEG XI, and an elephant's back tooth.

This was my world, a world I felt to be utterly secure and certain to last for ever. True, I couldn't trace myself back to Barbarossa – what Jew could? But I knew that the Schwarzes had been here in Stuttgart for at least two hundred years, perhaps much longer. How could one tell, when there were no records? How was one to know where they had come from? – Kiev or Wilna, Toledo or Valladolid? In what derelict graves between Jerusalem and Rome, Byzantium and Cologne were their bones rotting? Could one be sure they had not been here before the Hohenfels? But these were questions as irrelevant as the song David sang to King Saul. All I knew then was that this was *my* country, *my* home, without a beginning and without an end, and that to be Jewish was fundamentally no more significant than to be born with dark hair and not with red. Foremost we were Swabians, then Germans and then Jews. How else could I feel? How could my father feel otherwise? Or my father's grandfather? We were not poor "Pollacken" who had been persecuted by the Czar. Of course we could not and would not deny that we were "of Jewish extraction", any more than anybody would dream of denying that my uncle Henri, whom we had not seen for ten years, was one of the family. But this "Jewish extraction" meant little more than that once a year, on the Day of Atonement, my mother would go to a synagogue and my father would neither smoke nor travel, not because he believed in Judaism but because he didn't want to hurt other people's feelings.

I still remember a violent discussion between my father and a Zionist who had come to collect money for Israel. My father abhorred Zionism. The whole idea seemed to him stark mad. To claim Palestine after two thousand years made no more sense to him than the Italians claiming Germany because it was once occupied by the Romans. It could only lead to endless bloodshed and the Jews would have to fight the whole Arab world. And anyway what had he, a Stuttgarter, to do with Jerusalem?

When the Zionist mentioned Hitler and asked my father if this would not shake his confidence, my father said, "Not in the least. I know my Germany. This is a temporary illness, something like measles, which will pass as soon as the economic situation improves. Do you really believe the compatriots of Goethe and Schiller, Kant and Beethoven will fall for this rubbish? How dare you insult the memory of twelve thousand Jews who died for our country? *Für unsere Heimat?*"

When the Zionist called my father a "typical assimilant", my father answered proudly, "Yes, I am an assimilant. What's wrong with it? I want to be identified with Germany. I should certainly favour the complete absorption of the Jews by the Germans if I could be convinced it would be of lasting profit to Germany, but I have some doubts. It seems to me that the Jews, by not completely integrating themselves, still act as catalysts, enriching and fertilizing the German culture as they have done in the past."

Here the Zionist jumped up. This was more than he could bear. Tapping his forehead with his right index finger he said in a loud voice: "Total *meschugge*", collected his pamphlets and disappeared, still tapping his forehead with his finger.

I had never seen my father, who was usually quiet and peaceable, so furious. For him, this man was a traitor to Germany, the country for which my father, twice wounded in the First World War, was quite ready to fight again.

10

HOW WELL I understood (and still understand) my father. How could he, or anyone else in the twentieth century, have believed in the Devil and in Hell? Or in evil spirits? Why should we exchange Rhine and Mosel, Neckar and Main for the sluggish waters of the Jordan? For him, the Nazis were no more than a skin-disease on a healthy body, and all one had to do was to give a few injections, keep the patient quiet and let nature follow its course. And why should he worry? Wasn't he a popular doctor, respected by Jews and Gentiles alike? Hadn't a deputation of eminent citizens led by the Mayor called on him on his forty-fifth birthday? Hadn't the *Stuttgarter Zeitung* printed his picture? Didn't a group of Gentiles serenade him with *Eine Kleine Nachtmusik*? And hadn't he got an unfailing talisman? The Iron Cross, First Class, hung over his bed and his officer's sword next to a picture of the Goethe-Haus in Weimar.

II

M<small>Y MOTHER WAS</small> too busy to bother about Nazis, Communists and other such unpleasant people, and if my father had no doubts that he was a German, my mother, if possible, had even fewer. It simply didn't enter her head that any sane human being could question her right to live and to die in this country. She came from Nuremberg where her father, who was a lawyer, had been born, and she still spoke German with a Franconian accent (she would say *Gäbelche*, little fork, instead of *Gäbele*, and *Wägelche*, little carriage, instead of *Wägele*). Once a week she would get together with her friends, mostly wives of doctors, lawyers and bankers, to eat home-made chocolate and cream cakes *mit Schlagsahne*, drink endless coffees *mit Schlagsahne* and gossip about servants, family matters and plays they had seen. Once a fortnight she went to the Opera and once a month to the theatre. She found little time for reading, but occasionally came to my room, looked longingly at my books, took one or two from the shelf, dusted them and put them back. Then she would ask me how I was getting on at school, to which, in a gruff voice, I always answered "all right", and she would leave me, carrying off any socks that needed mending or shoes due for repairs. Occasionally, with a nervous movement, she put a hand tentatively on my shoulder, but she did this more and more rarely, sensing my resistance to even such mild demonstrativeness. Only when I was ill did I find her company acceptable and surrendered gratefully to her repressed tenderness.

12

I THINK MY parents were very good physical specimens. My father, with his high forehead, grey hair and short-clipped moustache, had an air of distinction, and was so little "Jewish" in appearance that once in a train an S.A. man invited him to join the Nazi Party. And even I, her son, couldn't help seeing that my mother, never very dressy, was a handsome woman. I have never forgotten how once, when I was a boy of six or seven, she came into my room to kiss me goodnight. She was dressed for a ball and I stared at her as if she had been a stranger. I clutched her arm, refused to let her go and started crying, which upset her very much. Could she have understood then that I wasn't unhappy or ill, that my trouble was seeing her objectively for the first time in my life as an attractive creature in her own right?

When Konradin came in I led him to the staircase, meaning to take him straight to my room without first introducing him to my mother. I didn't then know precisely why I did this, but it's easier for me today to realize why I tried to smuggle him in. Somehow I felt he belonged to me and to me alone, and I didn't want to share him with anybody. And probably – and this makes me blush even now – I felt my parents weren't "grand" enough. I had never been ashamed of them – indeed, I had always felt rather proud of them, and now I was horrified to discover that because of Konradin I was behaving like a beastly little snob. For a second I almost disliked him because I realized he was responsible. It was his presence that was making me feel like this, and if I despised my parents I despised myself even more. But just as I reached the staircase, my mother, who must have heard my steps, called out to me. There was no escape. I had to introduce him.

I took him into our Persian-carpeted living room with its heavy oak furniture, blue Meissen plates and long-stemmed wine glasses in purple and blue on a dresser. My mother was sitting in the "Winter garden" under a rubber tree, mending a pair of socks, and she didn't seem the least bit surprised to see me and my friend. When I said "Mother, this is Konradin von Hohenfels" she looked up for a moment, smiled and gave him her hand, which he kissed. She asked him a few questions, mainly about school, his future plans, to what university he meant to go, and told him how pleased she was to see him in our house. She behaved just as I would have wished and I saw at once that Konradin was pleased with her. Later I took him up to my room where I produced all my treasures: my books, coins, the Roman fibula and the Roman tile with the inscription LEG XI.

Suddenly I heard my father's footsteps and he came into my room, something he hadn't done for months. Before I had time to introduce them, father clicked his heels together, stood stiffly, almost to attention, stretched out his right arm and said, "Gestatten, Doctor Schwarz". Konradin shook my father's hand, bowed slightly, but said nothing. "I am greatly honoured, Herr Graf," said my father, "to have the scion of such an illustrious family under my roof. I have never had the pleasure of meeting your father, but I knew many of his friends, particularly Baron von Klumpf who commanded the second squadron of the first Uhlan regiment, Ritter von Trompeda of the Hussars and Putzi von Grimmelshausen, known as Bautz. I am sure your Herr father must have told you of Bautz, who was a bosom friend of the Kronprinz? One day, so Bautz told me, His Imperial Highness, whose headquarters were then at Charleroi, called him and said to him: 'Bautz, my dear friend, I want to ask a great favour. You know Gretel, my chimpanzee, is still a virgin and badly needs a husband. I want to arrange a wedding to which I shall invite my staff. Take your car and travel around Germany and find me a healthy good-looking male.' Bautz clicked his heels together, stood to attention, saluted and said,

'Jawohl, Imperial Highness'. Then he marched out, jumped into the Kronprinz's Daimler and travelled from zoo to zoo. A fortnight later, he came back with an enormous chimp called George V. There was a fabulous wedding, everybody got drunk on champagne and Bautz got the *Ritterkreuz* with oak leaves. There's another story that I must tell you. One day Bautz was sitting next to a Hauptmann Brandt, who in civilian life was an insurance agent, but always tried to be '*plus royaliste que le roi*', when suddenly" – and so my father went on till at last he remembered that there were patients waiting for him in his surgery. Once more he clicked his heels together. "I do hope, Herr Graf," he said, "that in future this will be your second home. Please commend me to your Herr father." And beaming with pleasure and pride, nodding to me to show me how pleased he was with me, he left my room.

I sat down shocked, horrified, miserable. Why had *he* done this? Never had I known him to behave so outrageously. Never before had he mentioned Trompeda and the atrocious Bautz. And the ghastly chimpanzee story! Had he invented all this to impress Konradin, just as I, only in a more subtle way, had tried to impress him? Was he, like myself, a victim of the Hohenfels mystique? And how he had clicked his heels! For the benefit of a schoolboy!

For the second time in less than an hour I almost hated my innocent friend, who had transformed my father (by his presence alone) into a caricature of his true self. I had always looked up to my father. He seemed to me to have so many qualities I lacked such as courage and a clear head, and he made friends easily and did his job punctiliously and without sparing himself. It's true that he was reserved with me, and didn't know how to show his affection for me, but I *knew* that it was there and even that he was proud of me. And now he had destroyed this image and I had reason to be ashamed of him. How ridiculous he had looked, how pompous and servile! He, a man whom Konradin should have respected! This picture of him, heel-clicking, saluting, "Gestatten Herr Graf", this horrible scene would for ever eclipse the father-hero of the past. He would never be the same man for me again; never would I be able to look in his eyes again without feeling ashamed and sorry, and ashamed that I was ashamed.

I trembled violently and could hardly keep back my tears. I had only one wish: never to see Konradin again. But he, who must have understood what was going on in my mind, seemed to be busy looking at my books. If he hadn't done so, if at this moment he had talked to me, worse still if he had tried to console me, to touch me, I should have hit him. He had insulted my father, and exposed me as a snob who deserved this humiliation. But he instinctively did the right thing. He gave me time to recover and when after five minutes he turned round and smiled at me I could smile back between my tears.

Two days later he came again. Without being asked he hung his coat up in the hall and – as if he had done this his whole life – went straight into our living-room in search of my mother. She welcomed him again in the same friendly, reassuring way, hardly looking up from her work, exactly as she had done the first time and as if he were just another son. She gave us coffee and *Streusselkuchen*, and from then on he regularly appeared three or four times a week. He was relaxed and happy to be with us, and only the fear that my father would tell more Bautz stories spoiled my pleasure. But he too was more relaxed; he became more and more used to the boy's presence and in the end stopped addressing him as "Herr Graf" and called him Konradin.

13

Since konradin had been to my home I expected to be asked over to his, but the days and weeks passed by without an invitation. We always stopped outside the iron grille crowned by two griffons which carried the armorial shield of the Hohenfels, until he said goodbye, opened the heavy gate and walked up the scented, oleander-bordered path leading to the portico and the main entrance. He knocked lightly on the huge black door, the door slid silently back and Konradin disappeared as if for ever. Occasionally I waited for a minute or two, staring through the iron bars, hoping Sesame might open again and that he would reappear, beckoning to me to come in. But he never did, the door was as forbidding as the two griffons, which looked down on me, cruel and pitiless, their sharp claws and split tongues shaped like sickles ready to cut out my heart. Every day I suffered the same torture of separation and exclusion, every day this house which held the key to our friendship grew in importance and mystery. My imagination filled it with treasures: banners of defeated enemies, crusader swords, suits of armour, lamps which once had burnt in Isfahan and Tehran, brocades from Samarkand and Byzantium. But the barriers which kept me from Konradin seemed to be fixed for ever. I couldn't understand it. It was impossible that he, so careful to avoid giving pain, so thoughtful, always ready to make allowances for my impetuosity, my aggressiveness when he disagreed with my *Weltanschauung* – should have *forgotten* to invite me. And so, too proud to ask him, I became more and more worried and suspicious, and obsessed by the desire to penetrate the stronghold of the Hohenfels.

One day, just as I was going, he turned round unexpectedly. "Come in, you haven't seen my room," he said. Before I even had time to answer he pushed the iron gates back, the two griffons receded, still threatening, but powerless for the moment and flapping their predatory wings in vain.

I was terrified, because I was unprepared. The fulfilment of my dreams had come so suddenly that for a moment I wanted to run away. How could I meet his parents with my shoes unpolished and a doubtfully clean collar? How could I face his mother, whom I had seen once from a distance, black against pink magnolias, her skin not white like my mother's but the colour of olives, her eyes the shape of almonds, her right hand rotating a white sunshade like a Catherine-wheel? But there was nothing I could do now except follow him, trembling. Exactly as I had seen it happen before, both in reality and in my dreams, he lifted his right hand and knocked gently at the door, which, obedient to his command, opened silently for him to enter and to admit me.

For a moment we seemed to be in complete darkness. Then my eyes gradually became used to it and I saw a large entrance hall, the walls covered with hunting trophies: enormous antlers, the head of a European bison, the creamy white tusks of an elephant whose silver-mounted foot served as an umbrella-stand. I hung up my coat and left my satchel on a chair. A servant came, bowed to Konradin. "Der Kaffee ist serviert, Herr Graf", he said. Konradin nodded and led the way up a dark oak staircase to the first floor, where I got a glimpse of closed doors, oak-panelled walls with a picture of a bear hunt, another of stags fighting, a portrait of the late king and a view of a castle which looked like a cross between Burg Hohenzollern and Neuschwanstein. From there we went up to the second floor and along a corridor where there were more pictures: *Luther before Charles V, The Crusaders entering Jerusalem,* and *Barbarossa asleep in the Kyffhäusser mountain,* with his beard growing through a marble table. One door was open; through it I saw a lady's bedroom with a dressing table covered with small bottles of scent and tortoiseshell brushes inlaid with silver. There were photos in silver frames, mainly of officers, but one looked almost like Adolf Hitler, and this gave me quite a shock. However, I had no time to investigate, and anyway I knew I was mistaken, for what would a photo of Hitler be doing in the bedroom of a Hohenfels?

At last Konradin stopped, and we went into his room which was rather like my own, only bigger. It had a fine view of a well-kept garden with a fountain, a small Doric temple, and a statue of a goddess covered with yellow lichen. But Konradin gave me no time to contemplate the landscape. He rushed to a cupboard and, with an eagerness that showed me how long he had been waiting for this occasion, his eyes shining in anticipation of my envy and wonder, he laid out his treasures. Out of their cotton wool he took his Greek coins: a Pegasus from Corinth, a Minotaur from Knossos, coins from Lampsagus, and Agrigentum, Segesta and Selinunte. But this wasn't all; other treasures followed, more precious than any of mine: a goddess from Gela in Sicily, a small bottle from Cyprus the colour and shape of an orange, with geometrical designs on it, a Tanagra figure of a girl wearing a chiton and a straw hat, a Syrian glass bowl iridescent as an opal, prismatic like a moonstone, a Roman vase the colour of milky pale-green jade and a small Greek bronze figure of Hercules. It was touching to see his delight at being able to show me his collection and to watch my amazement and my admiration.

The time passed incredibly quickly and when two hours later I left, I had neither missed his parents nor particularly considered that they might have been away from home.

14

ABOUT A FORTNIGHT later he asked me again. Again we went through the same pleasant routine: we talked, looked, compared, admired. Again, too, his parents seemed to be away, which I really didn't mind, as I was rather scared of meeting them, but when this happened a fourth time I began to suspect that it was no coincidence and to be afraid that he only invited me when his parents weren't there. Though I felt a little hurt, I didn't dare to ask him about it.

Then one day I remembered the photograph of the man who looked like Hitler – but immediately felt ashamed that I could even for a moment have suspected my friend's parents of having any connection with such a man.

15

Bᴜᴛ ᴛʜᴇʀᴇ ᴄᴀᴍᴇ a day when no more room was left for doubt.

My mother had got me a ticket for *Fidelio* with Furtwängler conducting, and I was sitting in the stalls waiting for the curtain to go up. The violins began to tune up, to hum, an elegant crowd filled one of Europe's most beautiful opera houses, and the president of the Republic himself was honouring us with his presence.

But hardly anybody looked at him. All eyes turned towards the door by the front row of the stalls, through which, slowly and majestically, the Hohenfels made their entrance. With a shock of surprise and some difficulty I recognized my friend, a strange, elegant young man in a dinner jacket. He was followed by the Countess, dressed in black with a glittering tiara of diamonds, a diamond necklace and diamond earrings, which shed a bluish light over her olive skin. Then came the Count, whom I now saw for the first time, grey-haired, grey-moustached, a diamond-studded star shining on his heart. There they stood, united, superior, expecting people to stare at them open-mouthed as by a right which nine hundred years of history had conferred upon them. At last they decided to move to their seats. The Count led the way, followed by the Countess, the aurora borealis of her diamonds dancing round her beautiful head. Then came Konradin who, before sitting down, looked round at the audience, bowing when he recognized anybody, as sure of himself as his father. Suddenly he *saw* me, but without giving me the slightest hint of recognition, then his eyes wandered round the stalls and up to the balconies and back again. I say he *saw* me, for I was sure that when his eyes met mine he had registered my presence. Then the curtain rose and the Hohenfels and the rest of us lesser folk were plunged into darkness until the first interval.

As soon as the curtain fell and without waiting for the applause to die down, I went into the foyer, a grand assembly room with Corinthian marble columns, crystal candelabra, gold-framed mirrors, cyclamen-red carpets and wallpaper the colour of honey. Here, leaning against one of the columns and trying to look haughty and disdainful, I waited for the Hohenfels to appear. But when at last I saw them I wanted to run away. Wouldn't it be better to avoid the thrust of the dagger which, I knew, with the atavistic insight of a Jewish child, would in a few minutes be plunged into my heart? Why not avoid pain? Why risk losing a friend? Why demand proof, instead of letting suspicion be lulled to sleep? But I had not the strength to run away, so steeling myself against pain, trembling, leaning against the column for support, I prepared myself for execution.

Slowly and majestically the Hohenfels came nearer and nearer. They walked abreast, the Countess in the middle, nodding to acquaintances or waving her bejewelled hand with a gentle, fan-like movement, the aurora of diamonds round her neck and head spraying her with beads of light like crystalline water drops. The Count inclined his head slightly to acquaintances and to the president of the Republic, who responded with a deep bow. The crowd gave way for them, and their regal procession went on unchecked, superb, and ominous.

They still had ten yards to go before they came up to me who wanted to know the truth. No escape was possible. Then five yards, then four separated us. Suddenly he saw me, he smiled, his right hand went up to his lapel as if he wanted to remove a speck of dust – and they had passed by. On they solemnly paced as if following the invisible porphyry sarcophagus of one of the Princes of the Earth, to the measure of some inaudible funeral march, smiling all the time and raising their hands as if they wanted to bless the crowd. When they reached the end of the foyer I lost sight of them, but a minute or two later the Count and Countess came back – without Konradin. Passing and re-passing they accepted the homage of the spectators.

When the bell rang for the second act I left my post, went home and, without being seen by my parents, straight to bed.

That night I slept badly. I dreamt that two lions and a lioness attacked me, and I must have screamed because I woke up to see my parents bending over my bed. My father took my temperature but couldn't find anything wrong with me, and the next morning I went to school as usual, though feeling weak as if I'd had a long illness. Konradin hadn't arrived; I went straight to my place, pretended to be correcting some homework and didn't look up when he came in. He went straight to his place too, and started arranging his books and pencils without looking at me. But as soon as the bell had gone for the end of the lesson he came up to me, put his hands on my shoulders – something he had never done before – and asked me a few questions, though not the most obvious one, whether I had enjoyed *Fidelio*. I answered as naturally as I could, and at the end of the school day he waited for me and we walked home together as if nothing had happened. For half an hour I kept up the pretence, but I knew perfectly well that he knew what was going on in me, or he would not have kept off the subject of the greatest importance to us both; the evening of the day before. Then, just when we were about to part and the iron gates were swinging to, I turned to him and said:

"Konradin, why did you cut me yesterday?"

He must have been expecting the question, but even so it came as a shock to him. He blushed and then went pale. Perhaps he had hoped that after all I wouldn't ask it, and that after a few days of sulking I would forget what had happened. One thing was clear, he was not prepared for me to speak out, and he started stammering something about his "not having cut me at all", about my "imagining things", being "hyper-sensitive", and he "not having been able to leave his parents alone".

But I refused to listen. "Look, Konradin," I said, "you know perfectly well that I'm right. Do you believe I didn't realize that you only invited me to your home when your parents were out? Do you really believe that I was imagining things last night? I must know where I stand. I don't want to lose you, you know . . . I was alone before you came and would be still more alone if you threw me over, but I can't bear the idea of your being too ashamed of me to introduce me to your parents. Understand me. I don't care about meeting your parents socially – except just once, just for five minutes, so as not to feel I'm an intruder in your home. Besides, I'd rather be alone than humiliated. I am as good as all the Hohenfels in the world. I tell you, *nobody shall* humiliate me, no king, no prince, and no count."

Brave words, but I was now almost in tears and could

hardly have gone on when Konradin interrupted me. "But I don't *want* to humiliate you. How could I? You know you're my only friend. And you know that I like you more than anyone else. You know that I have been lonely too and that if I lose you I shall lose the only friend I can trust. How could I have been ashamed of you?" Doesn't the whole school know about our friendship? Didn't we travel around together? Did it ever occur to you before that I was ashamed of you? And you dare to suggest a thing like that!"

"Yes," I said, now much calmer. "I believe you. Every word. But why were you so different yesterday? You could have talked to me for a second and could have acknowledged my existence. I wasn't expecting much. Just a greeting, a smile, a wave of your hand would have been enough. Why are you so changed when your parents are there? Why haven't I been allowed to meet them? *You* know *my* mother and father. Tell me the truth. There must be a reason why you haven't introduced me to them and the only reason I can think of is that you're afraid your parents will disapprove of me."

He hesitated for a moment. "All right, then," he said, "*tu l'as voulu, Georges Dandin, tu l'as voulu.* You want the truth, you shall have it. As you saw, and how could *you* of all people not have seen it, I didn't *dare* to introduce you. The reason, I swear by all the gods, has nothing to do with being ashamed – there you're wrong – it is far simpler and more unpleasant. My mother comes of a distinguished – once royal – Polish family, and she hates Jews. For hundreds of years Jews didn't exist for her people, they were lower than the serfs, the scum of the earth, untouchables. She detests Jews. She's afraid of them though she has never met one. If she were dying and nobody but your father could save her, I'm not sure she'd call him in. She'll never consider the idea of meeting you. She's jealous of you because you, a Jew, have made a friend of her son. She thinks my being seen with you is a blot on the Hohenfels escutcheon. She's afraid of you, too. She believes you have undermined my religious faith, and that you are in the service of world Jewry, which is only another word for Bolshevism, and that I'll be a victim of your devilish machinations. Don't laugh, she's serious. I have argued with her, but all she says is: 'My poor boy, don't you see that you are already in their hands? You already talk like a Jew'. And if you want the whole truth, I've had to fight for every hour I've spent with you; and the worst of all, I didn't dare talk to you last night because I didn't want to hurt you. No, my dear friend, you have no right to reproach me, no right whatever, I tell you."

I stared at Konradin who, like me, was greatly disturbed. "And your father?" I stammered.

"Oh, my father! That's different. My father hardly cares whom I meet. For him, a Hohenfels will always be a Hohenfels wherever he is and whomsoever he meets. Perhaps if you were a Jewess it might be different. He'd suspect you of wanting to hook me. And he wouldn't like that at all. Of course, if you were immensely rich he *might*, she *just* might consider a marriage possible – but even so he'd hate to hurt my mother's feelings. You see, he's still very much in love with her."

Until now he had managed to be calm, but suddenly, carried away by emotion, he shouted at me: "Don't look at me with those stricken dog's eyes! Am I responsible for my parents? Is any of it my fault? Do you want to blame me for the ways of the world? Isn't it time we both grew up, gave up dreaming and faced reality?" After this outburst he grew calmer. "My dear Hans," he said with great gentleness, "do accept me as I have been created by God and by circumstances which I can't control. I've tried to hide all this from you, but I should have known that I could never deceive you for very long, and I ought to have had the courage to talk to you about it before. But I'm a coward. I simply couldn't bear to hurt you. But I'm not completely to blame; you do make it very hard for anyone to live up to your ideas of friendship! You expect too much from simple mortals, my dear Hans, so do try to understand and forgive me, and let's go on being friends."

I gave him my hand, not daring to look in his eyes, because one or both of us might have started crying. After all we were only sixteen years old. Slowly Konradin shut the iron gates which were to separate me from his world. I knew and he knew that I could never cross the frontier again and that the House of the Hohenfels was closed to me for ever. Slowly he walked up to the door, lightly touched a button and the door slid back silently and mysteriously. He turned back and waved to me, but I didn't wave back. My hands were gripped round the iron bars like those of a prisoner crying for release. The griffons, their beaks and claws like sickles, looked down on me, holding high and in triumph the armorial shield of the Hohenfels.

He never asked me to his home again and I was grateful he had the tact not to. We met as before, as if nothing had happened, and he came to see my mother, but less and less often. We both knew that things would never be the same again and that it was the beginning of the end of our friendship and of our childhood.

16

AND THE END wasn't long in coming. The gale which had started blowing from the east now reached Swabia too. It grew in violence to the force of a tornado and didn't abate until, some twelve years later, Stuttgart was three-quarters gutted, medieval Ulm a heap of rubble and Heilbronn a shambles in which twelve thousand people had perished.

When I went back to school after the summer holidays, which I spent in Switzerland with my parents, grim reality penetrated the Karl Alexander Gymnasium for the first time since the First World War. Until then, and for much longer than I could realize at the time, the school had been a temple of humanities into which the Philistines had never yet managed to introduce their technology and their politics. Homer and Horace, Euripides and Virgil were still more important here than all the inventors and temporary masters of the world. True that over a hundred of the boys had been killed in the last war, but this was what had happened to the Spartans at Thermopylae and to the Romans at Cannae. To die for one's country had been to follow their time-honoured example.

> Noble is he who falls in front of battle
> bravely fighting for his native land
> and wretched the man who begs, a recreant
> city-less, from fertile acres fled.

But to take part in *political* strife, this was another story. How could we have been expected to follow today's events when our history masters never taught us about anything that had happened later than 1870? How could they, poor devils, squeeze into the two hours per week allotted to them the Greeks and Romans, the Holy Roman Emperors and the Swabian kings, Frederick the Great, the French Revolution, Napoleon, and Bismarck? Of course, even we could not by now be altogether unaware of what was going on outside the temple. There were huge, blood-red posters all over the town denouncing Versailles and the Jews; swastikas and the hammer and sickle disfigured the walls everywhere, and long processions of the unemployed marched and counter-marched through the streets; but as soon as we were inside again time stood still and tradition took over.

A new history master, Herr Pompetzki, arrived in the middle of September. He came from somewhere between Danzig and Königsberg which made him probably the first Prussian ever to teach at the school, and his clipped, sharp diction sounded strange to the ears of boys used to the broad, lazy Swabian dialect.

"Gentlemen," he began his lecture, "there is history and history. History which is in your books now and history which soon will be. You know all about the first, but nothing about the second because certain dark powers which I hope to tell you about have an interest in keeping it hidden from you. For the moment, anyway, let's call them 'dark powers', powers which are at work everywhere, in America, in Germany, but particularly in Russia. These powers are more or less cleverly disguised, influencing our way of life, undermining our morals and our national heritage. 'What heritage?' you will ask. 'What are you talking about?' Gentlemen, is it not incredible that you should have to ask? That you have not heard of the priceless gift that has been bestowed on us? Let me tell you what this heritage has meant in the last three thousand years. Round about 1800 BC, some Aryan tribes, the Dorians, appeared in Greece. Until then Greece, a poor, mountainous country, inhabited by people of an inferior race, was asleep, impotent, the home of barbarians with no past and no future. But soon after the arrival of the Aryans the picture changed completely until, as we all know, Greece blossomed out into the most brilliant civilization in the history of mankind. Now let us advance in time. You have all heard how the Dark Ages followed the fall of Rome. Do you believe it can have been pure chance that soon after the German Emperors' descent on Italy the Renaissance began? Or isn't it more than probable that it was German blood that fertilized the fields of Italy, barren since the fall of Rome? Can it be a coincidence that the two greatest civilizations were born so soon after the arrival of the Aryans?"

So he went on for one hour. He carefully avoided naming the "dark powers", but I knew and everybody knew whom he meant and as soon as he had left a violent discussion broke out in which I took no part. Most of the boys agreed that it was all rot. "What about the civilization of China?" Frank shouted. "And the Arabs? And the Incas? Hasn't he ever heard of Ravenna, the idiot?"

But some, mainly the duller boys, said there was something in his theory. What other reason could there have been for the mysterious rise of Greece so soon after the Dorians got there?

But whatever the boys thought about Pompetzki and his theories, his coming seemed to have changed the whole atmosphere overnight. Until then I had never met with more animosity than one normally gets among boys of different classes and interests. Nobody seemed to have strong views about me, and I hadn't run into any religious or racial intolerance. But when I got to school one morning, I heard the noise of a violent discussion through the closed door of my classroom. "The Jews," I heard, "the Jews." These were the only words I could distinguish, but they recurred like a chorus and there was no mistaking the passion with which they were being uttered.

I opened the door, and the discussion stopped abruptly. Six or seven of the boys were standing in a group. They stared at me as if they had never seen me before. Five of them shuffled away to their places, but two – Bollacher, the inventor of Castor and Pollack, who had hardly spoken to me for a month, and Schulz, an aggressive lout who weighed a good twelve stone, the son of a poor village pastor and destined to follow in his father's footsteps – looked me straight in the eye. Bollacher grinned, the kind of superior stupid grin which comes over some people's faces when they see a baboon at the Zoo, but Schulz, holding his nose as if there was a bad smell, stared at me provocatively. For a moment I hesitated. I felt I had at least half a chance of downing this great clod, but didn't see that it would help matters much if I did. Too much poison had already seeped into the school atmosphere. So I went to my place and pretended I was having a last look at my homework – like Konradin, who had an air of being too busy to have eyes and ears for what was going on.

Now Bollacher, encouraged by my failure to take

up Schulz's challenge, rushed towards me. "Why don't you go back to Palestine where you came from?" he shouted, and taking a small piece of printed paper out of his pocket he licked it and stuck it on my bench in front of me. It said: "The Jews have ruined Germany. People, awake!"

"Take it away," I said.

"Take it away yourself," he said, "only mind: if you do I'll break every bone in your body."

Here was the crunch. Most of the boys, including Konradin, got up to see what was going to happen. This time I was too frightened to hesitate. It was do or die. I hit Bollacher in the face as hard as I could. He staggered, then came back at me. Neither of us had any science; it was rough-and-tumble – yes, but it was also Nazi vs. Jew, and I was fighting in the better cause.

My passionate sense of this mightn't have been enough to see me through if Bollacher, swinging a blow at me which I dodged, hadn't tripped and got himself wedged between two desks at the precise moment when Pompetzki himself came in. Bollacher picked himself up. Pointing at me, with tears of mortification running down his cheeks, he said: "Schwarz attacked me."

Pompetzki looked at me. "Why did you go for Bollacher?"

"Because he insulted me," I said, trembling with rage

71

and the strain of it all.

"He insulted you? What did he say?" asked Pompetzki softly.

"He told me to go back to Palestine," I answered.

"Oh, I see," said Pompetzki with a smile, "but that's not an insult, my dear Schwarz! It's sound, friendly advice. Sit down, both of you. If you want to fight, fight outside as much as you like. But do remember, Bollacher, that you've got to be patient. Soon all our problems will be solved. And now back to our history lesson."

When evening came and it was time to go home, I waited until everybody had gone. I still had some faint hope that *he* would be waiting for me, would help me, would console me, now when I needed him most. But when I left, the street was as cold and empty as a beach on a winter day.

From then on I avoided him. It would only have embarrassed him to be seen with me and I expected he would be grateful for my decision. I was alone now. Hardly anyone spoke to me. No longer did Muscle Max, who had taken to wearing a small silver swastika on his jacket, ask me to show my paces. Even the old teachers seemed to have forgotten me. I was rather glad of it. Already the long, cruel process of uprooting had begun, already the lights which had guided me had grown dim.

17

ONE DAY AT the beginning of December I had come home tired, when my father took me into his surgery. He had aged in the last six months and seemed to have some difficulty in breathing. "Sit down, Hans, I want to talk to you. What I say now will come to you as a shock. Mother and I have decided to send you to America, for the time being anyway, till the storm has blown over. There are our relations in New York who'll look after you and arrange for you to go to university. We believe this will be best for you. You haven't told me what's going on at school, but we can imagine that it has not been easy for you. At a university it would be even worse. Oh! – the separation won't be for long! Our people will come to their senses in a few years' time. As far as we ourselves are concerned, we shall stay. This is our Fatherland and our home and we belong to it, and we won't let any 'Austrian dog' steal it from us. I'm too old to change my habits. But you are young, you have your whole future before you. Now don't make any difficulties, don't argue, or it will be all the harder for us. And for God's sake don't talk for a bit."

And so it was settled. I left school at Christmas and on January 19th, my birthday, almost exactly a year after Konradin had come into my life, I left for America. Two days before my departure I got two letters. The first one was in verse, the joint effort of Bollacher and Schulz:

> Little Yid – we bid you farewell
> May you join Moses and Isaac in hell.

> Little Yid – where will you be?
> Joining the Jews in Australie?

> Little Yid – never come back
> Or we'll break your bloody neck.

The second ran:

My dear Hans,

This is a difficult letter. First let me tell you how very sad I am that you are leaving for America. It can't be easy for you, who love Germany, to start a new life in America – a country with which you and I have nothing in common, and I can imagine how bitter and unhappy you must feel. On the other hand it's probably the wisest thing you can do. The Germany of tomorrow will be different from the Germany we knew. It will be a new Germany under the leadership of the man who is going to determine our fate and the fate of the whole world for hundreds of years to come. You will be shocked when

I tell you that I believe in this man. Only he can save our beloved country from materialism and Bolshevism, only through him can Germany regain the moral ascendancy she has lost by her own folly. You won't agree, but I can't see any other hope for Germany. Our choice is between Stalin and Hitler and I prefer Hitler. His personality and sincerity impressed me more than I should ever have thought possible. I met him recently when I was in Munich with my mother. Outwardly he is an unimpressive little man, but as soon as one listens to him one is carried away by the sheer power of his conviction, his iron will, his demonic intensity and prophetic insight. When my mother left she was in tears and kept on repeating: "God has sent him to us." I'm sorrier than I can say that for a time – perhaps a year or two – there won't be a place for you in this New Germany. But I can't see any reason why you shouldn't come back later. Germany needs people like you and I am convinced that the Führer is perfectly able and willing to choose between the good and the undesirable Jewish elements.

> For that which dwells near its origin is reluctant
> to leave the place

I am glad your parents have decided to stay here. Of course nobody will molest them and they can live and die here in peace and security.

Perhaps one day our paths will cross again. I shall always remember you, dear Hans! You have had a great influence on me. You have taught me to think, and to doubt, and through doubt to find our Lord and Saviour Jesus Christ.

Yours Konradin v. H.

18

Aᴎᴅ ꜱᴏ ɪ came to America. I have been here for thirty years.

When I got here I went to school and then on to Harvard, where I studied law. I hated the idea. I wanted to be a poet, but my father's cousin was standing no nonsense. "Poetry, poetry," he said, "do you think you're another Schiller? How much does a poet earn? First you study law. Then you can write as much poetry as you like in your spare time."

And so I studied law, became a lawyer at the age of twenty-five and married a girl from Boston by whom I have one child. As a lawyer I have done "not too badly" as the English say, and most people would agree that I've made a success of things.

Superficially they are right. I have "everything" – an apartment overlooking Central Park, cars, a place in the country, I belong to several Jewish clubs and so on. But I know better. I have never done what I really wanted to do: to write a good book and *one* good poem. At first I lacked the courage to set about it because I had no money, but now that I have the money I lack the courage because

I have no confidence. So, in my heart of hearts I look on myself as a failure. Not that this really matters. *Sub specie aeternitatis* we all, without exception, are failures. I don't know where I read that "death undermines our confidence in life by showing that in the end everything is equally futile before the final darkness." Yes, "futile" is the right word. Still, I mustn't grumble: I have more friends than enemies and there are moments when I am almost glad to be alive – when I watch the sun set and the moon rise, or see snow on mountain tops. And there are other compensations, as when I am able to throw what weight I have on the side of a cause I consider good – racial equality for instance, or the abolition of capital punishment. I have been glad of my financial success because it has made it possible for me to do a little to help the Jews to build up Israel and the Arabs to settle some of their refugees. I have even sent money to Germany.

My parents are dead, but I am glad to say that they didn't end in Belsen. One day a Nazi was posted outside my father's surgery carrying this notice: "Germans, beware. Avoid all Jews. Whoever has anything to do with a Jew is defiled." My father put on his officer's uniform together with his decorations, including the Iron Cross, First Class, and took up his stand beside the Nazi. The Nazi got more and more embarrassed, and gradually quite a crowd collected. At first they stood in silence, but as their numbers increased there were mutterings which finally broke into aggressive jeers.

But it was at the Nazi that their hostility was aimed and it was the Nazi who, before long, packed up and made off. He didn't come back nor was he replaced. A few days later, when my mother was asleep, my father turned on the gas; and so they died. Since their death I have, as far as possible, avoided meeting Germans and haven't opened a single German book, not even Hölderlin. I have tried to forget.

Of course a few Germans have inevitably come my way, good fellows who were in prison for fighting Hitler. I made sure about their past before shaking hands with them. You have to be careful before you can accept a German. How do you know that the man you are talking to hasn't dipped his hands in the blood of your friends and relations? But in these cases there was not the slightest doubt. In spite of their own records of resistance they were apt to have a sense of guilt, and I felt sorry for them. But even with them I pretended that speaking German was an effort for me.

It is a kind of protective façade that I put up almost (though not quite) unconsciously when I have to talk to a German. Of course I can still speak the language perfectly well, allowing for my American accent, but I dislike using it. My wounds have not healed, and to be reminded of Germany is to have salt rubbed into them.

One day I met a man from Württemberg and I asked him what happened to Stuttgart.

"Three-quarters destroyed," he said.

"What happened to the Karl Alexander Gymnasium?"

"Rubble," he said.

"And the Palais Hohenfels?"

"Rubble."

I laughed and laughed.

"What are you laughing at?" he asked with amazement.

"Never mind," I said.

"But there's nothing funny about it," he said. "I can't see the joke!"

"Never mind," I repeated. "There is no joke." What else could I have said? How could I have explained to him why I laughed when I myself cannot understand?

19

Now all this came back to me today when out of
the blue an appeal arrived – together with a little book
of names – from the Karl Alexander Gymnasium, asking
me to subscribe for a war memorial to the boys who had
fallen in the Second World War. I don't know how they
got my address. I can't understand how they found out
that, a thousand years ago, I had been "one of them". My
first impulse was to throw it all into the wastepaper
basket: why should I bother about "their" death: I had
nothing to do with "them", absolutely nothing. That part
of me had never been. I had cut seventeen years out of
my life without asking "them" for anything and now
"they" wanted a contribution from *me*!

But in the end I changed my mind. I read the appeal;
four hundred of the boys had been killed or were missing.
Then there was the list of their names in alphabetical
order. I went through it, avoiding the letter H.

"ADALBERT, Fritz, killed in Russia 1942." Yes, there
had been a boy of this name in my class. But I couldn't
remember him, he must have been as insignificant
to me in life as he was now in death. The same with

the next name, "BEHRENS, Karl, missing in Russia, presumed dead."

And these were boys whom I might have known for years, who were once alive and full of hope, who laughed and lived as I had done.

"FRANK, Kurt." Yes, I remembered *him*. He was one of the three Caviars, a nice boy, and I felt sorry for him.

"MULLER, Hugo, died in Africa." I remembered him too; I closed my eyes and my memory produced, like a faded daguerreotype, the vague, blurred outline of a blond boy with dimples, but that was all. He was just dead. Poor chap.

It was different with "BOLLACHER, dead, grave unknown." He deserved it – if anybody deserved to be killed (and "if" is the operative word). And so did Schulz. Oh, I remembered *them* well. I had not forgotten their poem. How did it start?

> Little Yid, we bid you farewell
> May you join Moses and Isaac in hell.

Yes, *they* deserved to be dead! – *If* anyone deserved it.

So I went through the whole list except the names beginning with H, and when I had finished I found that twenty-six boys out of the forty-six in my class had died for *das 1000-jährige Reich*.

And then I put the list down – and waited.

I waited for ten minutes, for half an hour, all the time looking at this printed matter emanating from the hell of my antediluvian past. It had come uninvited, to disturb my peace of mind and rake up something I had tried so hard to forget.

I did a little work, made some phone calls, dictated a few letters. And still I couldn't either let the appeal alone or force myself to look up the one name that haunted me.

At last I decided to destroy the atrocious thing. Did I really want or need to know? What difference would it make if he were dead or alive, since dead or alive I should never see him again?

But could I be certain? Was it completely and utterly out of the question for the door to open and for him to walk in? And wasn't I even now listening for his footstep?

I took hold of the little book and was on the point of tearing it up, but at the last moment held my hand. Steeling myself, trembling, I opened it at the letter H and read,

"VON HOHENFELS. Konradin, implicated in the plot to kill Hitler. *Executed.*"